LOST LITTLE LEOPARD

ALSO BY W. BRUCE CAMERON

Bailey's Story

Bella's Story

Ellie's Story

Lily's Story

Max's Story

Molly's Story

Shelby's Story

Toby's Story

Lily to the Rescue

Lily to the Rescue: Two Little Piggies

Lily to the Rescue: The Not-So-Stinky Skunk

Lily to the Rescue: Dog Dog Goose

Lily to the Rescue: Lost Little Leopard

Lily to the Rescue: The Misfit Donkey

W. BRUCE CAMERON

LILY TO THE RESCUE

LOST LITTLE LEOPARD

Illustrations by

JAMES BERNARDIN

A TOM DOHERTY ASSOCIATES BOOK

NEW YORK

This is a work of fiction. All of the characters, organizations, and events portrayed in this novel are either products of the author's imagination or are used fictitiously.

LILY TO THE RESCUE: LOST LITTLE LEOPARD

A Starscape Book
Published by Tom Doherty Associates
120 Broadway
New York, NY 10271

www.tor-forge.com

The Library of Congress Cataloging-in-Publication Data
is available upon request.

ISBN 978-1-250-76256-6 (trade paperback)
ISBN 978-1-250-76259-7 (hardcover)
ISBN 978-1-250-76260-3 (ebook)

First Edition: February 2021

Printed in the United States of America

0 9 8 7 6 5 4 3 2 1

Dedicated to the people saving animals at the Humane Society of the United States.

LOST LITTLE LEOPARD

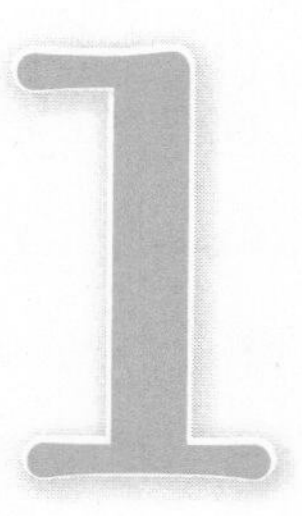

I was playing in the backyard with my girl, Maggie Rose, and my good friend Brewster.

Well, Maggie Rose and I were playing. Brewster was watching. Watching is something Brewster does a lot.

Napping is something he does even more.

Maggie Rose is my girl, and I am her dog. We were playing my favorite game in the entire world, which is Give-Lily-a-Treat. But Maggie Rose kept getting it wrong.

"Play dead, Lily," she told me. "Play dead!"

She had that treat clutched tight in her fist. I knew it was in there! Her whole hand smelled like chicken, and chicken is the best treat. No, maybe salmon. No, bacon . . . or peanut butter. . . . These are the sorts of things I think about a lot, but I never can make up my mind.

Probably the best treat of all is whichever one I'm about to eat, so I nibbled and licked at Maggie Rose's fingers, trying to get to that chicken-smelling thing she was clutching so tightly.

Brewster lay next to us in the grass. Brewster is a lot older than I am, and a lot lazier. He and I often go to a place called Work, where I visit animals and he sleeps. Then we go Home, where I play with Maggie Rose and he sleeps. He was interested in the treat, too, but not interested enough to get up and do anything about it.

That's how he is. I don't understand it, but there are lots of things I don't understand—like why Maggie Rose wasn't giving me the treat! I licked her hand even harder, trying to get my tongue between her fingers.

"No, Lily!" Maggie Rose told me.

Humans like that word: "No." I do not.

Maggie pushed me away a little. "Play dead, Lily!" she told me.

I stared at her. She had that tone in her voice that she uses when she wants me to do a trick, like Sit or Down or Shake. But she wasn't saying any of those words.

Still, when I do Sit or Down or Shake I get a treat sometimes. So I tried. I put my rump on the grass and looked eagerly at Maggie Rose.

She didn't give me the treat. So I flopped down to put my belly in the grass. Treat now, right?

Maggie Rose did not seem to notice how well I was doing Down. So I jumped up to give her my paw. Everybody likes it when I do Shake. Maggie Rose couldn't possibly resist and would give me chicken!

Except she didn't.

Brewster let out a long sigh and rolled over so that he could rub his back in the soft grass. He wiggled a little and groaned as the warm sun touched his belly. He closed his eyes.

"Good dog, Brewster!" Maggie Rose exclaimed. "Good job playing dead!"

Then she gave Brewster my treat.

I stared at her in dismay. Brewster got a treat for, what, taking a nap? Brewster takes naps all the time, whether anybody tells him to or not! It isn't a trick!

I don't think Brewster knew why he was getting chicken any more than I did, but he ate it. I jumped into Maggie Rose's lap and licked both her hands to get all the chicken taste I could. Since she was my girl, I accepted that she gave my treat to Brewster.

Good dogs have to put up with a lot of unfair things.

While I was working on Maggie Rose's hands, Mom came out into the backyard. I like Mom very much and normally I would run over to sniff at her shoes and see if she smelled like any new animals. Mom goes to Work every day and there are lots of animals at Work.

But I was too busy getting the last traces of chicken off Maggie Rose's thumb, so I only wagged my tail in Mom's direction.

"Maggie Rose," Mom said. "Your dad just called. He's working up in the mountains today, and he needs Lily."

"Why?"

"I don't know. He just said to bring you both, a bottle of kitten formula, and he'd explain when we got there."

Then Maggie Rose and Mom did the thing that people do sometimes, where they hurry around saying stuff like "Where's my phone?" and "Maggie Rose, tie your shoes, please!" I helped by following Maggie Rose closely so that she'd know I was always there if she needed anything. I am so good at this that she even tripped over me a few times.

When we got to the car, Casey fluttered down and landed on the ground. Casey is both my friend and a crow. He croaked up at me. "Ree-ree," he said. He says this a lot when I am around. It sounds a little like *Lily*.

"Can we bring Casey, Mom?" my girl asked.

"Better not. We don't know what your dad is doing, and I wouldn't want Casey to get in the way."

Sometimes Mom lifts the back of the car and Casey flies right in, into one of the cages back there. But not this time. Casey wasn't coming, and neither was Brewster, who was probably still lying down in the backyard, waiting for another treat to fall on him for doing nothing.

When I climbed into the back seat with Maggie Rose I sniffed to confirm she still had chicken. She did! I could tell she had treats making a delicious bulge in her pocket.

As we drove, I put my nose out of the window and sniffed as hard as I could. That's what I love best about car rides—all the smells that come gushing in the window, so many that they make me sneeze. Maggie Rose likes to wipe her face after I sneeze.

Soon the air coming at me was cleaner and colder.

I turned away from the window so I could sneeze on her cheek.

"Lily!" Maggie Rose sputtered.

I wagged.

The car stopped and Maggie Rose let me out. I squatted and made a puddle in the worn-out grass, then looked around, excited to be here even though I didn't know where I was or what we were doing.

I saw some big buildings, bigger than the house where I lived with Maggie Rose. Next to the buildings were big patches of lawn that had been fenced in. I hoped I'd get to go into one of those yards soon, and be off my leash and maybe find another dog to wrestle with.

"James!" Mom waved at Dad, who had just come out of a building. "We're here!"

He walked over to us, and I tugged on the leash to drag Maggie Rose closer so I could smell his shoes. He has the best shoes, even better than Mom's, with thick soles packed full of marvelous odors.

Dad gave Mom and my girl a hug and reached down to pet me. "You want to see something special?" he asked my girl.

Then I heard a scream.

2

"What was that horrible noise?" my girl asked in alarm.

Dad grinned. "Come on, I'll show you." We followed Dad around the side of a building. Maggie Rose clapped her hands in excitement. "They're so pretty! So red!"

Birds! Big birds in cages, much bigger than Casey. One of them let loose with a piercing shriek and I blinked in surprise. Casey says "Ree-ree" and makes other noises, but never such a loud screech. “What are they?” my girl asked.

“Scarlet macaws,” Mom replied. “What

are they doing here, James?" She calls Dad "James" sometimes, which is odd because his name is Dad. Even a dog knows that.

Dad wore a disgusted expression. "The guy who lives here has been smuggling exotic animals. We came up with a warrant to arrest him. Those macaws must have been brought up from South America. They're wild, and they definitely don't belong in the Rocky Mountains. Macaws are jungle birds, accustomed to living in large rainforests. They wouldn't survive the winter—if we hadn't come along, they would have been sold illegally to collectors who would keep them in indoor cages for the rest of their lives."

I sensed that Maggie Rose was upset. I left Dad's shoes and went to sit close by her legs. I touched her knee with my nose so she'd remember she had a good dog with her. "Why would anyone do that, Dad?" she asked.

Dad sighed. "People will sometimes do bad things for money, Maggie Rose."

"It's why we need game wardens like your father, to protect the animals," Mom added.

One of the big birds let out another screech. I expected that someone would shout "No!" but nobody did.

"Wow," Maggie Rose exclaimed. She looked at Dad. "What's going to happen to the macaws now? Will they have to go to a zoo?"

Dad shook his head. "No, they're better off being released back into the wild, where they belong. We've been on the phone with the government in Veracruz, where there's a preserve, and we're going to take them there. But that's not why I asked your mom to bring you and Lily up here, Maggie Rose. The man we just arrested wasn't just smuggling birds."

"What else was he up to?" Mom asked.

"Jungle cats," Dad replied. "We got a tip

that he was trying to sell some tiger cubs, but that's not what we found. There's only one kitten here—a very scared little leopard who needs some help."

Dad led us to a tall fence with a gate in it. Dad opened the gate and we all entered a smaller yard. He shut the gate behind us.

The situation called for a ball or a squeaky toy, and I gazed expectantly at my girl.

"Where is it?" Maggie Rose asked Dad.

"See the pile of big boulders? She has a den up in there in one of the cracks."

"How big is it, James?" Mom wanted to know.

"She's just a baby, but I didn't really get a good look at her." Dad looked down at Maggie Rose. "Do you think Lily can get the leopard cub to come out? I really don't want to have to crawl in there after her. She's already scared."

"Lily can make friends with anybody," Maggie Rose proclaimed confidently. She bent down and snapped the leash off my collar. "Go get the leopard, Lily. Go on. Go!"

I was excited to be off leash and dashed around the yard. Whatever we were doing, it was fun!

"Lily, you silly," my girl called to me. I trotted up to her, thinking how much a chicken treat would improve things, but she made no move to dig into her pocket. She squatted down and pointed at some big rocks. "In there, Lily. Go see the baby leopard."

No toys, no treats. But my girl obviously wanted me to do something. When she gestured with her hand, as if throwing something at the rocks, I moved in that direction, puzzled but willing to play.

And that's when I smelled a familiar smell—the smell of a cat.

I know a lot about cats. When I go to Work

with Mom, there are usually cats there. They live in crates, like all the animals at Work, and people come to meet the cats and then, if they're lucky, take the cats home. The *really* lucky people get to go home with dogs.

That is what happened to me. I used to live at Work, and now I live at Home with Maggie

Rose. It happened to Brewster too—he came home to be with my girl's brother Bryan.

But before the animals go Home with their new people, I play with them. I play with cats and puppies and grown-up dogs and sometimes with my friend Freddy the ferret.

Would I be able to play with this new cat? Sometimes cats are afraid of dogs, even a good dog like me or a napping dog like Brewster. This might be one of those scared cats, because it wasn't coming out. I could tell it was young, a girl kitten, and an unfamiliar smell clung to it—different than any animal I'd ever met.

"Go on, Lily," my girl urged. "Go find the leopard!"

Whatever my girl wanted from me would have to wait—I was too interested in the smell of the hidden cat!

I bounded forward and stuck my nose into the crack between two round boulders. Yes, she was hiding in there, and I could tell she was frightened and alone.

I have met lots of animals who are afraid of me at first. I know what to do about that, and how to help them calm down so they can play.

I thought about squirming into the space between the rocks, but I knew that would really scare her. Instead, I made myself smaller by lying down on my belly.

"Good dog, Lily," Maggie Rose praised.

There was a slight movement way back in the darkness. I saw the kitten hiding in the shadows. She was a pretty large kitten! She was staring at me. I wagged, still lying down. Doing Down was how I usually helped the cats at Work see I was not a threat.

Brewster had gotten a treat for lying down in the dirt. Now here I was doing the very same thing, but nobody was handing me a treat.

But wait . . . Brewster had *already* been lying down. He didn't get a treat until he rolled on his back.

Was that the secret?

I decided to try it.

3

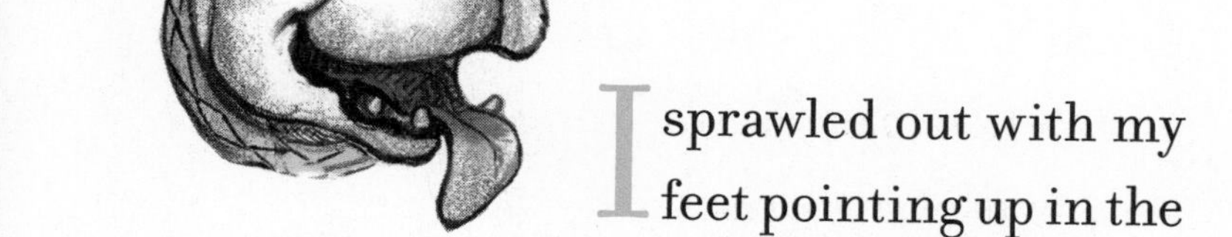

I sprawled out with my feet pointing up in the air, wiggling and wagging in a perfect imitation of Brewster. Maybe now my girl would give me some chicken!

Mom, Dad, and my girl didn't move. No treats dropped from the sky. But I noticed something—in the shadows, the large, scared kitten stirred.

I watched her tentatively come forward. Seeing an upside-down cat walk toward me made me a little dizzy, but I remained on my back.

As she approached, the sunlight fell across her face. Her fur was spotted and her chin was a light color, lighter than the rest of her. She thrust that nose out of the rocks in order to be able to smell the good dog who was doing Brewster's trick with no treats.

I sniffed back. I smelled catness, but that other, unknown smell was something more wild. She did not smell like a kitten who curls up in laps. She did not smell like a kitten who gets treats from her humans for doing no tricks at all, like most cats.

The kitten sniffed my face all over. She moved on to my head and neck, coming even farther out into the sun.

I held still, because I could tell that the kitten was still scared. I could see it in the stiff way she moved, in her wide eyes and her alert ears. She was ready to run away at any moment.

The kitten squeezed completely out of the crack so that she could sniff at my rump and tail. She glanced up at Mom and Dad and Maggie Rose, but didn't seem to care that they were there—they weren't moving, which might have been why the kitten wasn't reacting to them. I've often seen that cats only get worked up about things that are moving. They'll ignore a ball that isn't rolling but they'll jump on one that is.

I could not imagine being the sort of animal who would ever ignore a ball under any circumstances.

I carefully flopped over so I was lying on my side. The kitten stared at me with wide, strange-colored eyes. I was pretty sure she would pounce on me—that's what always happened with new cats at Work. So I was surprised when she lowered her head, rubbing her round ears along my ribs, and then cuddled up against me as if I were a mother cat.

"Look at that," I heard Dad say.

"Poor thing has been all alone and is starving for love," Mom said.

"Lily is such a good dog," my girl said. I wagged at the sound of her voice saying my name.

"Do you have the bottle?" Dad asked.

"Right here in my pack," Mom replied. "Come with me, Maggie Rose."

Having the large kitten pressed up against my side was making me drowsy, but I noticed when Mom and my girl walked a short distance from Dad to a different part of the yard. The kitten picked her head up, but didn't do anything else as they both sat down in the grass.

"Maggie Rose, call Lily, but very softly," Mom said.

"Lily? Come here, now," my girl said quietly. I moved my head to see her more clearly. What did she want?

"Come here now, Lily," she repeated. Oh, she was saying *Come.* I knew how to do Come. I climbed to my feet, mindful to do it gently so I wouldn't disturb the kitten, who watched me alertly.

When I trotted over to my girl, the kitten didn't move. The humans went very still.

"If she goes back to her den, I'll have to try to catch her with a net," Dad murmured. "Hate to scare her so badly, but we won't have a choice."

Mom had something in her hand. I pointed my nose in that direction. It was a bottle! I knew about bottles. I once had some young pig friends who liked to suck on bottles very much. I could smell that this bottle had milk inside it, and my mouth started to water. I did Sit.

"This isn't working," Mom said worriedly.

"Lily, can you play dead again? Play dead!" Maggie Rose urged. "Play dead!"

I held out my paw for a perfect Shake. My

girl didn't grab it. "Play dead!" she repeated. I put my stomach in the grass—a really great Down! Still no treat.

Then my girl reached out and rolled me gently onto my back. "Play dead!" she repeated.

Oh, the Brewster trick! I pointed my feet at the sky and Maggie Rose slipped me a chicken treat. I loved Maggie Rose!

Upside down, I could see the kitten was cautiously making her way toward us.

"Oh, little one, it's all right," Mom said very softly. "Here, look. I bet you want this. Don't you?" Still sitting on the lawn, she reached out both her hands, the one holding the bottle and the one that wasn't. There was a tiny drop of milk clinging to the tip of the bottle.

I started to wag, thinking that bottle would make a perfect reward for a dog doing Brewster's trick.

Mom and my girl weren't moving at all. The kitten sniffed the air, approaching slowly. Soon she was there, pressing her face against my side. Mom lowered the bottle, and the kitten touched it with her nose.

I didn't want this kitten getting any ideas about my bottle. I stretched my neck out to sniff it too. I was getting my tongue ready to lick off that little droplet of milk when Mom pushed my face away.

"No, Lily," she said.

I really wished humans would just forget the word "no." It never makes anyone feel good.

The kitten was still pressing against my side when she put out her scratchy tongue and closed her mouth around the tip of the bottle. I watched, utterly dismayed, as the kitten made small sucking noises. "That's right, baby," Mom whispered. "You're hungry, huh? I know you're hungry."

Mom gently pulled the bottle back toward her body. The kitten allowed herself to be led, leaving my side. The next thing I knew, the kitten was being cuddled on Mom's lap and sucking eagerly out of the bottle, while

I lay there in the dirt with no milk and no treat at all!

Apparently I was the only one upset about this unfortunate turn of events, because Mom and Maggie Rose were both smiling.

"Great job, you two," Dad said from the other side of the yard.

"And Lily," my girl reminded him.

"And Lily," he agreed.

Since they were all saying my name, I decided to get back on my feet. I shook myself off, casting an unhappy glance at the kitten, who was still sucking away on my bottle.

Dad was making his way very slowly and carefully toward us. Suddenly he jerked in alarm. "Oh no," he gasped.

4

"What's wrong, Dad?" Maggie Rose asked.

"This is the first I've gotten a good look at her," Dad said. "That's not just a baby leopard. That's an *Amur* leopard."

Mom's mouth dropped open. "Are you sure?"

Dad nodded.

"What's Amur mean?" my girl asked.

"It's the rarest of the big cats. There are

fewer than a hundred left in the wild. That makes this little kitten very, very important," Dad replied. He turned and went out the gate and was back a moment later with a big plastic crate. He set it on the ground and opened the door, backing away.

"I know!" Maggie Rose said brightly. "Let's put Lily in there first. That way the leopard won't be as afraid."

"Excellent idea," Mom said.

Dad grinned. "That's my game warden girl."

"Lily, come!" My girl put me in the crate, handing me a chicken treat as a reward. *Yes!*

"Stay!" Maggie Rose commanded.

I've never been very fond of Stay, but I sat in the crate.

"Down!"

It seemed to me I was being asked to do a lot of things for a single chicken treat, but

I went ahead and dropped to my stomach. Mom put the kitten in the crate. I sniffed her milk breath. She immediately curled up next to me, just like before.

Mom shut the gate. "All babies need to cuddle," she observed. "It's an instinct as strong as the need to eat."

I was not bothered when Dad picked up the crate, but the large kitten clearly didn't like it. She stared at me with wide eyes as if expecting me to do something about it. Dogs know people are completely in charge of the world, but most cats don't believe this.

When the crate stopped moving it was in the back of Mom's car. The kitten cowered when Mom opened the crate door.

"Come, Lily!" Maggie Rose called.

I jumped out but the kitten remained behind.

"Where are you taking the leopard?" Maggie Rose asked as Mom climbed into the front seat.

"To the zoo. There's a special place set aside for animals that need to be kept by themselves for medical treatment." Mom waved and then the car drove away.

Dad turned to smile at my girl. "Good thing I thought to ask you to bring Lily." He came over and scratched my back. I wiggled happily and panted up at him. Then I licked something very tasty off his left shoe.

I noticed some people, who I had learned to think of as friends of Dad, loading the big birds, one cage at a time, into two large trucks. It was a day for taking all sorts of animals for car rides.

"Let's head back, Maggie Rose. I've got a lot to take care of if I'm going to get those macaws back where they belong."

We climbed into Dad's truck. I sat with my head in Maggie Rose's lap and we started to move.

"Dad, will you take the baby leopard back to the rainforest, too?"

Dad shook his head. "No. Amur leopards are from cold areas—Russia and China. They're almost extinct. We can't risk losing a single one. She'll live in a zoo somewhere."

"That's a little sad," Maggie Rose said. She stroked my back. "Poor lost little leopard, living in a cage."

Dad nodded. "But not really a cage—it will be a large enclosure. When she grows up, she'll be able to have cubs of her own. We're trying to build up their numbers to the point where we can save the species."

"What will happen to the man who took the baby away from her mother?"

"That man," Dad replied grimly, "is going to spend time in a much, much smaller cage."

"She was so cute," Maggie Rose said. "And Lily liked her."

Dad chuckled. "Lily likes everybody. Thank goodness."

The next day, Maggie Rose and I took another car ride with Mom. Brewster decided to stay at Home, and Casey must have been busy doing crow things, because he was not around.

"Can I name her, Mom?"

"Who? The Rottweiler puppy we're going to rescue, or the leopard from yesterday?"

"Both!"

"The puppy already has a name: Jax. He's fourteen weeks old. Thankfully, he's had his shots, so we won't have to keep him separated from Lily."

"Okay. But I think the leopard's name should be Nala."

I glanced at Maggie Rose. What was a Nala?

"Perfect," Mom agreed.

"What happened to Jax's person?"

Mom sighed. "It's a sad story, actually. Jax was being fostered by a man named Owen, who is an army soldier. Owen fell in love with the puppy and asked if he could keep Jax forever."

"Foster failure," my girl noted.

"Exactly. But then Owen received orders to go to Korea for at least a year. He decided it made no sense to take a Rottweiler puppy, and he couldn't ask Jax to wait for him that long, so he dropped Jax off at his sister's house."

"That's horrible! Why would he go and leave his dog?" Maggie Rose demanded.

"Well, Owen has a duty to serve his country. Sometimes, that means sacrifice. But we all do things for the common good that aren't easy. Take your dad—he's going to Veracruz for almost two weeks. I'm sure he would rather stay home with us, but he needs to return those macaws to their natural environment."

"I'll miss Dad, but saving animals is the most important thing," my girl agreed.

"And sometimes saving animals is fun. Owen's sister is your friend Charlotte's mom. You can play a little when we get there."

We soon stopped at a house I had never smelled before. Maggie Rose and I jumped out of the car together. In the front of the house there was a tire hanging from a tree, and a girl hanging from the tire. She was leaning back so far that her dark hair brushed the grass. Then she sat up and waved.

"Hi, Charlotte!" Maggie Rose greeted her.

"Hi!" the girl answered. "My mom said you'd bring your dog. What's her name?"

"Lily," said Maggie Rose.

I wagged to hear my name, and the girl with the long dark hair flopped out of the tire and onto the grass. "Lily! You're so cute!" she said, and I ran over to lick at her face and sniff her hair.

Then I saw something over the girl's shoulder.

A cat! The cat was crouched under a bush near the house. She was staring at me with very wide eyes.

I hadn't really gotten to play with the large kitten the day before, so I was tremendously excited to meet this cat! I wiggled out of

New Girl's lap and bounded toward my new friend.

"Oh, Mia!" New Girl said. She sounded worried.

"Lily just wants to play," Maggie Rose told her.

"Mia doesn't really play. She's pretty mean. Like, *really* mean."

When I reached my new playmate, her ears went back on her head, her eyes squeezed into slits, and she hissed, her mouth opening on wicked fangs. I halted in shock. She lunged forward with one paw up over her head, and I scrambled back from her razor-sharp claws as they raked the air, and nearly my face.

What sort of game was *this*?

This was not a nice cat. This was a bad cat!

I backpedaled as Bad Cat came at me, slashing the air, hissing and spitting.

"Lily!" my girl called.

Bad Cat licked her paw and stared at me. I went to Maggie Rose, who had to be as outraged as I was at such behavior.

"Sorry," New Girl said. "Mia doesn't like dogs very much."

I followed my girl and New Girl into the house. Mom sat at a table and talked with another grown-up lady whose name also seemed to be Mom—at least that's what New Girl called her.

"We're going to go play with Jax!" New Girl announced.

"Okay, just don't let Jax inside the house," Other Mom Woman agreed. She looked at Mom. "Jax is a bit wild."

We crossed to a big sliding window. I wagged because I could see a young dog sniffing along a fence in the backyard.

“Ready? One, two, three. . . . Go!” New Girl said.

The door slid open, we all jumped out, and the door thumped shut. The puppy raised its black face and stared at me.

“Jax! You have a new friend!” New Girl called.

This dog was named Jax, and I could smell he was a young male—much younger than I had thought, because he was so big. He came running across the yard in the half-tripping way puppies have, and I wagged, ready for him to stop so we could sniff each other’s butts.

Jax did not stop.

He crashed into me, almost knocking me over. He was heavy. As he jumped up on me, his legs pressed down and I squirmed away. I tried to push him over and he pushed back.

“That’s a big puppy!” my girl exclaimed.

I tried to run away and Jax was right there, bumping into me, nearly plowing me over. He was clearly too young to know I should be in charge—I should be the one crashing into *him,* if I chose.

I finally managed to wrestle Jax onto his

back, but he was hard to pin down. He was very strong.

After a time, Mom slid the door open and came out with a leash for the puppy. I was relieved—playing with Jax had left me exhausted.

"Bye, Charlotte!" Maggie Rose called.

We left the yard through a gate. As we approached the car, I saw Bad Cat glaring at me from the base of a tree. Jax saw him too and lunged to the end of his leash, yanking on Mom's arm. "Whoa! Jax, calm down."

Bad Cat acted as if the sight of two dogs didn't scare her.

We went to Work. Along the way, Mom said, "I'm going to need to spend a little time training Jax before we find a home for him. Usually Rottweilers are very even-tempered—they were originally used to herd animals and pull carts like horses. That's why they are so strong. But Jax doesn't seem to have gotten the message that Rotties are supposed to be calm and obedient."

"Lily's obedient," Maggie Rose observed.

"Yes, she is."

My girl slipped me a chicken treat and I crunched it gratefully.

At Work, Jax was led, twisting and pulling at the end of his leash, back into the area where the kennels were. My girl and I played Book, where she sits with a dry, tasteless thing in her lap and tickles it. I do not understand why anyone would want to play with such a boring object when there are squeaky toys in the world.

I was soon snoozing, but lifted my head when Mom walked up.

"Maggie Rose," she said. "There's a big problem with the leopard."

"With Nala?" My girl set her book toy aside.

My girl was worried. I got to my feet, ready to help.

Mom reached down and smoothed back the fur on my head. I licked her fingers. They smelled like Jax. "Nala isn't eating. She's been hiding behind some rocks since I dropped her off. What do you think, should we see if Lily can help?"

On the car ride I could sense that my girl was worried, so instead of sticking my nose out the window or watching for squirrels, I cuddled with her.

Maggie Rose asked, "Is Nala sick?"

Mom shrugged. "I examined her pretty carefully, but yes, she could be sick. Or maybe she's just upset at everything that's going on. We don't know where she came from, or how she got here."

"Or maybe she's lonely," Maggie Rose suggested. "She's all alone."

"Or she's lonely," Mom agreed.

When we stopped and my girl opened the door, I was astounded at the mix of odors that drifted across the parking lot toward me. The very strong smell of many animals was on the air—mostly animals I had never sniffed before.

Maggie Rose loves all animals. Surely if we met some new ones, she would no longer be so worried. I pulled Maggie Rose right across the parking lot, heading straight for these smells.

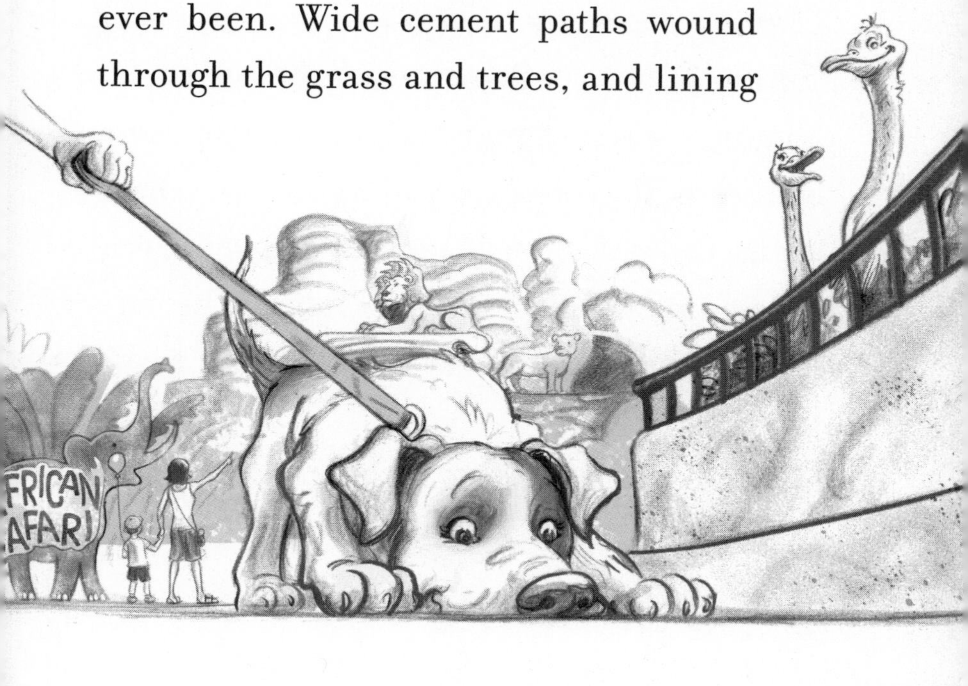

We passed through some gates and soon were in the most amazing place I had ever been. Wide cement paths wound through the grass and trees, and lining these paths were huge kennels, all of which were filled with the intense smell of different animals. I zigzagged back and forth on my leash, towing Maggie Rose behind me, sniffing madly.

Mom turned away from us. "Let me just take this call." She put her phone to her face.

Maggie Rose pulled me over near a fence. "Giraffes! See the giraffes, Lily?"

On the other side of the fence, very large non-dogs were eating leaves from tall trees. *Extremely* large non-dogs. They were so big I did not want to look at them. Dogs prefer small creatures to play Chase-Me and other games with, like cats and squirrels. These animals were too tall to be of use to any dog. I knew their feelings would be hurt if I ignored them but it was their fault for being so big.

"Maggie Rose!" Mom called, "We have to go!"

Mom came striding briskly up to us, shaking her head. "I'm sorry, honey, this is all my fault," she apologized. "The animals here shouldn't be exposed to dogs. Dogs are usually prohibited from even being here. Lily's allowed because she's got a job to do, but we can't let her approach anything but the leopard. Stay on the path. You could look at the fish ponds, I suppose—I doubt the fish would be upset to see a dog. But everything else is off-limits."

"Okay, Mom."

"Did you know the zoo already has Amur leopards?" Mom asked as we walked along.

"They do?"

"They are a mating pair: Dazma, the female, and Hari Kari. They're old for leopards, now—thirteen. They have the most amazing blue-green eyes."

"So Nala doesn't have to be lonely after all?"

Mom smiled. "Well, it's not so simple. Dazma and Hari Kari would not welcome a cub who was not theirs. And there are so few Amur leopards in the world that Nala, when she's old enough, will join a breeding program at some other sanctuary."

I found a patch of melted ice cream that I licked up off the ground. What a great place!

"This way," Mom said. We climbed some steps—I found a French fry!—and entered through some doors and into a building that smelled like people and unknown animals.

We stopped outside a gate that was made entirely of bars set close together. Through the bars, I could see a small sort of yard with a high fence all around it.

A man with dusty pants was waiting for us there. "Hello, Doctor Quinton," Mom said.

"So good of you to come on such short notice, Chelsea," the man with dusty pants replied. "And this must be Maggie Rose and Lily. Which is which?"

Mom laughed.

"My dog is Lily. I'm Maggie Rose," my girl said seriously.

"Well, I do appreciate you bringing your dog, Maggie Rose. I hope Lily can coax our new little leopard to come out."

"I named her Nala," Maggie Rose informed Dusty Pants.

"Nala! What a nice name. We'll call her that for now," he agreed.

Mom swung the pack from her back and dug inside it. A moment later she pulled out a bottle that smelled like milk. I stared at it. What a delightful idea!

"Come, Lily." Mom took my leash from Maggie Rose and led me through that door. My girl and Dusty Pants stayed on the other side, but I could see her through the bars.

There was sand under my feet, and a pile of boulders in a corner, and a small pool. I ignored the pool because I don't like to swim and I *especially* don't like baths. I glanced at the bottle of milk, wondering when we were going to put it to good use.

All the animal smells floating past my nose were so overpowering it was hard to sort out one from another. But I suddenly realized I had previously smelled one scent in particular.

It was a cat. It was young. It was frightened.

It was the large kitten I had met the day before. Instantly, I had a very bad feeling that I knew who the milk bottle was for.

"Nala!" Mom called softly. "Nala, baby, come and see who's here!"

Nothing happened.

"Nala!"

I scratched at my ear so that the tags on my collar jingled. Then I glanced back at Maggie Rose, who was standing with Dusty Pants at the gate, her hands clutching the bars. "Do you want to let Lily see if she can find Nala?"

"Let Nala come out on her own," Mom replied softly.

It occurred to me that they were saying "Nala" because that was the name of the large kitten. This might be where she lived now—her scent was certainly painted all over everything.

I yawned and then blinked in surprise. Nala the large kitten was suddenly standing on top of a big boulder, looking down at us with her light eyes and spotted face. I wondered who had helped her climb up there.

"It's okay, Nala. Remember Lily?"

Mom bent down and snapped the leash off my collar. I stretched, unsure what we were doing. Was I supposed to go play with the cat on the rock? Or stay with Mom and the bottle?

I picked Mom.

Then Nala dropped silently from her perch, landing lightly on all four feet. "Leopards are amazing jumpers," Mom said over her shoulder to my girl.

Nala sat at the base of the big rock and stared at me. I reminded myself that this wasn't like Bad Cat, this was a kitten who liked me. Wagging, I wandered up to sniff her face and was rewarded with a swipe on my snout.

I wish cats would learn that jabbing a dog in the nose is no way to play.

Nala lowered her front legs to the ground and left her rump up high in the air, wig-gling. I have played with lots of cats, so I knew exactly what she was going to do next. She pounced at me, but I was ready! I dodged to one side and nudged her with my head.

She toppled over into the dirt, lying on her back and kicking with both legs. I jumped on her so that I could gently chew her face and her ears. She shoved me off with her strong back feet.

Nala knew Wrestling! I raced around the

yard to see if she knew Chase-Me, too, but she didn't seem to. She just waited for me to run back to her and jumped on my back, hugging me tight with her front legs.

I flopped down so we could roll in the dirt, and then I looked up to see that Mom was sitting down on the ground. "Lily? Bring your friend over here. Come, Lily."

I obediently made to go to Mom, but Nala was right at my side, leaping up onto me, so I was a bit distracted. Eventually, though, we both closed the distance between us and Mom, and then Nala stopped, looking at Mom with unblinking eyes.

For some reason, Nala did not understand that Mom loved all animals. I went to Mom and nosed her and she petted my head, and then I looked pointedly at the bottle in her hand.

"It's okay, baby," she said. "Remember me?"

Nala solemnly watched me rubbing my head on Mom. When I flopped down on my belly and put my head in Mom's lap, Nala took a small step forward. Then another, and then another.

Maggie Rose made an excited sound on the other side of the door.

Mom held out the bottle of milk toward

Nala. By now I'd figured out who the milk was for—not a deserving dog, that was for sure. Humans often make decisions that make no sense to dogs.

Nala stared at the bottle. Her nose wiggled. Her whiskers trembled. She came closer and closer, and Mom pulled the bottle back a little at a time until Nala had to climb right into her lap to get it. I moved my head so Nala wouldn't step on it.

Nala grabbed hold of the bottle with her two front paws. She sucked and sucked.

When there are no treats being offered, a dog can always find ways to be happy. I ran around the yard. There was a stick in the dirt, and I grabbed it and shook it so hard it cracked.

Then the door opened. I looked up to see if it was Maggie Rose, but it wasn't.

Dusty Pants stepped through the gate, shutting it behind him. "That's amazing!" he marveled softly. "She wouldn't touch the milk this morning. I tried everything I could think of. Why does having Lily here make all the difference?"

Nala didn't even look up at him. I wagged, though, touching his Dusty Pants hand with my nose.

Mom nodded at me. "For some reason, my

daughter's dog just has the knack for putting animals at ease."

"I don't need to tell you how great this is. We were discussing force-feeding the cub, but that would only be a last resort. We need to keep her healthy, though, and she just hasn't wanted to eat."

"Mom," my girl called. "Can I come in and see Nala?"

The man and Mom exchanged glances. "Honey," Mom said, "we need to limit the number of people the leopard is exposed to. I'm sorry."

I spent most of the day at that wonderful place, called "Zoo." Most of the time was spent wrestling with Nala. Some of the time was spent watching Mom give Nala bottles of milk, and some of the time I sat with Maggie Rose on the other side of the gate.

When we arrived back at Home, Brewster

was there but Dad was not. I sniffed curiously, wondering where he was.

"I miss Dad, too," Maggie Rose told me. "He's in Veracruz right now, Lily. He's staying in a hotel right near the jungle, and he says he can hear monkeys in the morning!"

The next morning I went to Work with Mom and Maggie Rose. My girl went to the cat area and began cleaning cages.

Jax was so excited to see me he was whining in his kennel. Mom put a leash on the puppy, who lunged and twisted, trying to get at me. Remembering the sensation of having his thick body crash into my ribs, I remained just out of reach.

In the yard, Mom reached into a pouch on her waist and pulled out some delicious treats. Jax, now off leash, tried to climb on my head.

"Jax, come," Mom said.

I went obediently to Mom and did Sit. Jax bit my face. "Jax," Mom urged gently. "Come. See how good Lily is?"

We spent a long time in the yard. I demonstrated over and over how to do Come. Jax demonstrated how to chew on my body, climb on Mom, roll on the ground, and run away when Mom tried to put him back on the leash.

Once inside Work, Jax saw Maggie Rose carrying a cat. He went crazy trying to get to it, leaping and pulling at the end of his leash. My girl twisted away and I put myself between her and Jax to protect her.

"No, Jax," my girl said.

"Jax doesn't seem to know about cats. I'm surprised—I would have thought Charlotte's cat Mia would have taught him a few lessons," Mom said as she struggled with the puppy.

"Charlotte said the cat lives in the house and front yard and Jax always stayed in the back," Maggie Rose replied.

Jax didn't earn himself a single treat that day. I received several, however, which almost made having Jax slam his body into me worth the whole ordeal.

After putting Jax in his kennel, we returned to Zoo. Wonderful smells! I gobbled up a piece of hot dog I found in the grass. And then Mom and I entered Nala's yard. Maggie Rose stayed behind the bars. The kitten was hiding again, but soon after I sniffed around the base of the big boulders, she emerged from behind the rocks.

"The same thing happened," Dusty Pants informed Mom. "Nala hasn't eaten since you left yesterday. She wouldn't even show herself. I'm very concerned."

"I'm hoping our little leopard will get used to her surroundings soon," Mom replied.

Nala liked to play all the usual cat games—Hide-and-Pounce, Wiggle-Your-Butt, and Roll-and-Wrestle. I'm very good at these games, because I play them with the not-so-large kittens at Work. Those kittens are fragile and I'm always careful with them, but when Nala and I did Wrestling, it was like playing with a dog.

When Mom produced a bottle, Nala followed me over to her lap, but I did not want to sit and watch the kitten have more milk, so I trotted over to Maggie Rose. Dusty Pants was talking to her, and he opened the barred gate to let me out to see my girl.

"I'm going to take Lily to the fish pond," Maggie Rose told the man.

"That's fine, but otherwise please don't go anywhere else without a staff member or your mother," Dusty Pants replied.

My girl took me to a big bathtub. We stood behind a fence. "See the fish, Lily?" I knew what *fish* was, but couldn't smell any. But yes, if she was asking if I'd like some, I would be more than happy with that, though I like chicken better.

When we returned to Nala's yard, my girl sat on the cement behind the bars, and I put my head in her lap and prepared for a little afternoon snooze. She was quiet, too—we hadn't even announced to Mom that we were back.

I heard Mom talking to Dusty Pants. The man cleared his throat. "I wonder if you'd be willing to donate Lily to us."

Maggie Rose sucked in a breath, and I glanced up at her curiously.

"Give Lily to the zoo?" Mom looked surprised. "That's a big thing to ask, Doctor Quinton. My daughter loves Lily more than anything."

"Just hear me out. When your dog leaves, it's as if someone has thrown a switch. Nala hides and won't come out. We need to get Nala to accept feedings from other staff members, which isn't going to happen without Lily."

"How long would this last?"

The man sighed. "I have to be honest. Once the program determines where they want Nala to go, we're going to need to make the move as successful as possible. I can't see us accomplishing that without your dog."

My girl raised her hand to her mouth, but she was not eating.

"That could be more than a year, Doctor Quinton," Mom objected. "You're saying Lily would move with Nala to one of the sanctuaries?"

"I wouldn't ask if this weren't desperately important, Chelsea. We have to do whatever it takes to help this little Amur leopard survive. The world can't afford to lose even a single one."

There was a long silence. "I'll have to talk to Maggie Rose, you understand. I really care about what we're trying to achieve—but this would be very hard for my daughter."

Maggie Rose buried her face in my fur. I did not understand what was happening, but I knew she was sad, and a sad girl always needs her dog.

"Oh no, Lily," she murmured. "Oh no."

Dad was still not at Home when we returned. My girl's brothers Bryan and Craig were, though. Craig talked to his phone, calling it "Dad." Then Bryan did the same thing. So the phone was called Dad now? Much of what humans do makes no sense to a dog, but this one was particularly confusing. How could Dad be a phone? How was a phone going to wear his wonderful shoes?

The phone was passed to Maggie Rose.

"Hi, Dad," she said in a small voice.

"What's wrong, Sweetpea?" I heard Dad's voice say. I sniffed the air but he was nowhere nearby. My nose couldn't find him anywhere in the house.

"I just miss you. I really need to talk to you," my girl told the phone that was not Dad.

"Do you want to talk now? You can take it somewhere private, if something's bothering you."

Maggie Rose shook her head. "No, I want to talk in person."

The next morning, Mom talked to her phone. She did not call it "Dad." Maggie Rose glanced up at her when she said, "I was afraid of that."

When Mom put the phone in her pocket, my girl asked, "What's wrong, Mom?"

"Nala refused to come out of her hiding place all night, and she's still in there."

"She needs Lily," my girl said quietly. "Doesn't she?"

"Why the sad look, Maggie Rose?"

My girl shook her head. "I was just hoping Lily could go to the rescue with me and play with Jax."

Mom smiled. "Let's stop there on the way."

At Work I was let out into the yard and a few moments later Jax bounded out as Mom held the door open for him. I cringed as I watched him barrel across the yard, knowing he was planning to crash into me. At the last moment, I dodged out of the way and the puppy fell and rolled in the grass. I jumped on him to keep him pinned down, but he was so strong he was soon wriggling away from me. He leaped and twisted and jumped.

"Look at that energy!" Mom said.

I was becoming annoyed with his habit of running at me at full tilt and then running *into* me, showing no restraint at all. At one point I actually chopped at the air with my teeth, letting him know I needed him to back away so I could rest from his constant playing. He sat and gazed at me, puzzled—considering, for the first time it seemed,

that there was some other creature in the world except him.

That didn't last long.

When I wearily climbed into bed with Maggie Rose that night, I nearly groaned with relief to be lying on soft blankets. I opened my eyes, though, when she reached for me and pulled me to her, wrapping her arms around me in a sad hug.

How could a hug be sad?

"Oh, Lily, I am going to miss you so much," she murmured in my ear.

I spent the next several days playing gently with Nala at Zoo and being crashed into in the backyard by Jax. Maggie Rose was doing School—the word means she leaves early in the morning and comes back with books in the afternoon. Craig and Bryan were doing School as well. So I spent my time with Mom. Every day, we went to the zoo to see Nala and give her a bottle. At Work I tried to let her know I would rather nap with Brewster, but she said, "Come, Lily," and let me out in the yard for another wrestling match with Jax.

Mom was still trying to teach Jax tricks for treats, like "Sit" and "Come." Jax seemed to think Mom was saying, "Climb on Lily and bite her lips." Whenever we were in the building, he was on leash and I wasn't. He pulled and strained to get into the cat area as we passed it. "Jax, you're going to be a good dog someday. Just not today," Mom told him.

I hoped someone would soon arrive and take Jax away. That happens a lot at Work. Animals live there for a little while, and then they leave to go and live with happy people.

I wondered which people the big screeching birds had gone to live with, and if they slept in their person's bed like I slept in Maggie Rose's. I also wondered why any person would choose to have a big bird with a sharp beak instead of a dog.

After a few more days Dad finally came back, and his shoes smelled better than ever! Everyone hugged him and was very happy to see him. Maggie Rose whispered something in his ear, and he nodded.

"I think I'm going to take Maggie Rose and Lily for a walk," Dad announced.

Mom regarded him oddly. She looked between Dad and my girl. "Oh?"

"Sure. Just a father–daughter walk with my game warden girl."

I was very excited to feel my leash click into my collar, especially since Jax was nowhere to be found. "You come, too, Brewster," Dad said. "You need the exercise."

Brewster likes to stop at almost every tree and lift his leg, so we walked very slowly down the sidewalk, pausing often.

"What's on your mind, Maggie Rose?"

"I really missed you, Dad."

"I missed you, too, honey."

"Something happened while you were gone."

Dad looked down at her and lifted his eyebrows. "Oh?"

I politely sniffed where Brewster had just marked.

"Nala can't live without Lily. Everyone says so. She doesn't eat or even come out. And Doctor Quinton at the zoo says they need to adopt Lily and take her away to go live somewhere until Nala is grown up. Which could take a year!"

I sensed the distress coming off my girl, and gazed up at her in concern.

"Oh, Maggie Rose, I'm so sorry that you've been carrying this all by yourself. Why didn't you talk to Mom?"

"Because . . . because you're the game warden. This should be your decision."

"Oh." Dad stopped and bent over so he could look at my girl with serious eyes. "Maggie Rose, Lily is your dog. This isn't a decision for me to make."

My girl's hand came down to touch me. Even her fingers were sad. I licked them.

"Is Nala really that important, Dad?"

They resumed walking again. Brewster took this as a sign that he should lift his leg on a fence.

"Every Amur leopard is important, Maggie Rose, because there are so few left. We don't know where she was stolen from, and so far the man we have under arrest isn't talking. But if we don't build up their population, we're going to lose them, and that would be a loss for all the world."

Maggie Rose bit her lip. "Then I know what I have to do."

We walked in silence for a long time. Finally Dad said, “What do you mean by that, Maggie Rose?”

“You left us to go to the jungle to free the macaws, because that’s your duty, even though it was a sacrifice to travel all that way and be away from your family. Like a soldier doing his duty and asking Mom to find a home for Jax. And this is the most important duty of all, because Nala won’t survive without Lily. So even though she could be gone for more than a year, I have to let her go."

"That's my game warden girl," Dad replied softly. He put his arm around her, and she put her arm around me.

Maggie Rose was crying, though I had no idea why. I licked her face and she hugged me for a long time.

Later, the family all sat at the big table and ate, and I squeezed myself between Maggie Rose's legs and Bryan's, since they are the ones who drop bits of food most often.

"The macaws handled the travel very well," Dad said. "They're back in the rain-forest and I think they'll be fine."

Bryan let a bit of bread fall to the floor, and I pounced on it.

"That's wonderful. And Bryan, stop feeding Lily at the table," Mom said.

I heard "Bryan" and "Lily" and wagged

happily. Yes, I loved Bryan at the dinner table very much.

“So,” Mom said carefully, “how was your walk?”

Nobody answered.

"Maggie Rose? Why are you so quiet this evening?" Mom wanted to know.

More silence. Dad cleared his throat. "I think Maggie Rose has something important she wants to tell us."

My girl was sad. I hurried to her legs and pressed against them, so she'd know her dog was near.

"I know what Doctor Quinton said," Maggie Rose finally replied.

"What do you mean?" Mom asked.

"He said that Nala can't live without Lily. That we need to give Lily to the zoo so Nala will eat, and that when Nala gets old enough to go be in the program, Lily needs to go with her for a while."

"I didn't realize you overheard us. Why didn't you say something, Maggie Rose?"

"I needed to talk to a game warden," Maggie Rose explained.

"I see," Mom said.

"So if it's Lily's duty to go live with Nala, she can go. But when Nala can live without my dog, Lily comes home," my girl declared. "Okay?"

There was a long silence. "Wow," Craig said.

I could feel everyone being worried and unhappy and I did not know what to do about it.

"Oh, Maggie Rose," Mom finally said with a sigh.

After the day that Dad and his shoes came back, I started spending a lot more time at Zoo with Nala.

Maggie Rose didn't always come—usually on days when everyone said "School." On those days I would only see Maggie Rose for a little while in the morning, and then a few hours before dinner and in the evenings. Both times she seemed sad. Even when I grabbed one of my favorite toys out from under her bed—an old pair of Craig's socks tied together—and shook it in her face, she didn't smile like she normally did.

Jax, on the other hand, was *full* of energy. Every day he seemed bigger than he was the day before. And he still crashed into me as if he couldn't figure out how to stop.

"Jax went after a cat in a crate yesterday," Mom told Dad after my girl and her brothers left to do School. "We were processing an adoption and the woman put the crate down just as I was bringing Jax in from the yard. He went completely wild on me, trying to get through the bars."

"Some dogs just don't understand that cats can defend themselves," Dad replied.

"Jax sort of doesn't understand *anything*. He loves Lily, though."

At Zoo Nala and I played all the usual cat games, and we almost always ended up doing Curl-Up-with-Lily. After that, Nala would drink her bottle of milk. I pretended I didn't care that there was none for me. But I did.

People decide where dogs go and what dogs do, and right now they had decided I needed to visit Nala and play cat games and visit Jax and play dog-crashing-into-dog games. That was all fine, but I wished I could make my girl happy again.

My girl was so sad all the time that I gave up my post underneath Bryan's legs at dinner and always stayed right next to her, leaning against her for comfort. One such evening the family was eating vegetables, which I don't like, and spicy meat, which I do.

"I have news. About the Amur leopard," Dad announced.

I felt my girl grow suddenly anxious and I nosed her hand.

"We've got a home for her at the Land of the

Leopard National Park. She'll be transferred as soon as she's a little bigger."

"Is that close?" my girl replied quietly.

"I'm afraid not, Maggie Rose. It's in Russia."

My girl got up from the table and ran into her bedroom. I went with her. I pressed up against her and tried to make her feel better, even though I had no idea what was wrong.

The next morning, after everyone said "School," Mom took Jax and me out into the yard at Work. This day, though, we were both on leashes. Jax chewed my ears and jumped over me and our leashes were all tangled before we even made it out the door.

Once outside I smelled cat. Jax didn't, because he was too busy gnawing on my face. I shook him off as Mom unclipped his leash. "Jax, I don't think you ever met Mia."

I froze when I saw who was coldly watching us from across the yard.

It was Bad Cat.

Off leash, Jax scampered in circles, trying to entice me to play Chase-Me. Then he spotted the cat. Instantly he was charging joyously across the grass—planning, I supposed, to body-slam Bad Cat.

But Bad Cat had other ideas.

10

Bad Cat's eyes were slits and her mouth was open, her sharp teeth on clear display. Jax slowed because this was not the reaction he had been expecting. Suddenly, spitting and hissing, Bad Cat went after Jax, slashing at the air. Jax tumbled backward, fleeing, pure panic on his face. He was playing Chase-Me now, all right, but for Bad Cat it wasn't a game. Yelping, Jax tried to get away, but Bad Cat wouldn't let him. Finally the puppy ran and hid behind me, his tail down.

Bad Cat sat in the middle of the yard and smirked. She knew she wouldn't get any trouble from me, and Jax was trembling, peering around me at the threat.

"Now you understand about cats, don't you, Jax?" Mom said softly.

The next day Maggie Rose did School while I went to Zoo to play with Nala. Mom gave Nala a bottle, of course. "We're going to start you on solid food soon, little one," she told Nala. I hoped she was saying that the next bottle would go to a good dog.

After feeding the kitten, Mom went away and was gone for a while.

I was sitting on top of Nala and gently tugging at one of her ears with my teeth when I smelled Mom returning. With her was another smell, one that I instantly recognized. Nala pushed me off with her powerful rear legs, but I didn't want to do Wrestle more. I stared in disbelief at the gate to Nala's yard.

Oh *no*.

Mom opened the cage. She had Jax in her arms. He was wiggling with excitement and licking Mom's face and trying to tell her as plainly as he could that he wanted to get down and play.

Now, in all my time at Zoo, I'd never seen

or smelled another dog there. There were so many animals I couldn't even count all the smells that came to my nose, but I was the only dog, always.

Now there were two dogs here! What was going on?

Mom put Jax on the ground and he came bounding over for a game of Crash-into-Lily. Then he pulled up short.

He'd just seen Nala.

Nala, larger than Bad Cat, stared at Jax. Jax lowered his head and padded up to me, taking a long route that kept him far away from Nala. He nosed me, worried.

When Nala decided to investigate, Jax backpedaled away from her.

I decided to demonstrate to Jax that Nala was not like Bad Cat. I climbed up on her and instantly we were playing, Jax completely forgotten. I put Nala on her back and she wrapped her legs around me and twisted away. She jumped on me and I flopped over on the ground, doing Brewster's trick of pointing my feet into the air. Nala pounced on me.

Movement caught my eye. It was Jax. He was crawling forward on his belly, unable to resist playing, even if he was still worried Nala might be mean.

Nala and I both paused our wrestling and watched Jax. When he was close, I saw Nala's rump go into the air, and I knew what was going to happen next.

Pounce! It was a cat's favorite game. Jax backed away in alarm, but then seemed to understand. Nala just wanted to play. He carefully lifted a paw and that's all it took—now they were wrestling.

"Come here, Lily," Mom called gently.

I happily trotted over to the gate and Mom opened it. Then I sat and watched Nala and Jax tumble. Nala was underneath, but she

squirmed out and ran to her pile of boulders and in a single bound leaped to the top. Jax looked up at her in astonishment. Wagging, he yipped, and then Nala pounced on Jax and they were back to doing Wrestling.

I knew Nala well enough to be able to tell when she was getting tired. As far as I knew, Jax never got tired, but when he went to the pool for a drink of water, Mom said, "Okay, Lily, let's see if this worked."

Mom went into the cage and sat down, a familiar-smelling bottle in her hand. Jax joyously dashed over to see her, and Nala, unable to resist an animal running, pounced on him. Together they landed in Mom's lap,

and then Nala caught sight of the bottle and went limp.

Mom had to keep shoving Jax's face out of the way, but she was able to give Nala the whole bottle. While she was doing so, a man came up to stand next to me to watch. It was Dusty Pants. He had on different pants, but they were still dusty. Mom stood up and came over to us while Jax and Nala resumed playing.

"Hello, Chelsea," Dusty Pants said.

Mom smiled through the bars. "I realized that we were all so happy with how Lily relates to other animals, we didn't even think about whether another dog would do. I decided that Nala would probably play with any puppy."

"That you were able to feed our leopard proves that you were right," Dusty Pants agreed.

Mom turned and watched the cat and dog

play. "Lily was the runt of the litter. I started thinking about what will happen when Nala grows up—she'll be huge compared to Lily. But Jax has thick legs and enormous feet—he's going to be big, big enough to wrestle with an adult leopard." Mom turned back to Dusty Pants. "And yes, the zoo may adopt Jax. I'll even come out and continue to train him. He needs it."

Mom opened the gate. She knelt and put a leash into my collar with a *snick.* She smiled at me. "I know someone who is going to be very happy about all this," she told me.

"Lily!"

It was my girl! I wagged and shook myself off and went to the end of my leash to greet her as she ran up the cement path to where I was waiting at the gate. Dad was coming up behind her, grinning. She dropped to her knees and wrapped me in her arms.

I sighed in contentment. I loved Maggie Rose.

"Dad picked me up from school and brought me straight here," Maggie Rose said. "He said you have a surprise?"

Maggie Rose stood up. I gazed up at her fondly. Dad reached out and grabbed the hand of Dusty Pants. "Hello, Doctor Quinton."

"Good to see you again, James," Dusty Pants said.

"What's the surprise?" Maggie Rose asked.

"Look who is in the enclosure with Nala," Mom replied.

11

Jax!" Maggie Rose gazed up at her mother in wonder. "You put Jax in the cage with Nala?"

Mom nodded. "They're going to be great friends."

"Look at the two of them," Dad said. "Finally Jax has met his match."

We all watched Jax and Nala play for a while. I wondered if I should get back in there and really entertain everyone, but no one opened the gate.

"All right, I've got to get back to work," Dad said.

"Me, too," Mom agreed. "Maggie Rose? Do you want to come help me? We just got in some guinea pig babies, and we have to figure out which are the boys and which are the girls so we can separate them—we don't want more guinea pig babies!"

"Can Lily come, too?"

"Of course! Lily's your dog."

Maggie Rose was not sad anymore! I'd done it! I'd finally made my girl happy!

"Let's let Lily in to go say goodbye to Nala and Jax," Mom suggested.

"Can't we bring Lily back for visits?"

Mom shook her head. "I don't want to confuse things. Jax is Nala's dog now—he's not going back to the rescue, or anywhere else.

Soon Nala will forget all about Lily, which is what we want. Jax will go to Russia with her when she's old enough, and he'll be her companion for life."

Mom opened the gate and I slipped inside. Nala and Jax had fallen into an exhausted heap and were cuddled up for a nice nap together. Nala picked up her head to watch me approach, but Jax didn't stir.

The way Maggie Rose was acting gave me the feeling that I would not get to see Nala again.

This happens to me sometimes. I will get to know another animal and even love that animal, but then my girl will be in a wistful mood and steer me to touch noses one last time, and then the animals have to leave for different places to live different lives.

It happened to me first with my mother and brothers and sisters. It happened to me with a squirrel that I knew named Sammy, and a skunk that Maggie Rose called Stinkerbelle, and a couple of piglets, and a lot of baby geese who thought I was their mother.

I don't really understand it. Sometimes I wish all my animal friends—Stinkerbelle and Casey and Nala and the piglets and all the baby geese (even though they were a little annoying at times) could just come Home and live there. We'd all have bowls in the kitchen for our own food and we'd all sleep in Maggie Rose's bed, cuddled up with her legs.

But that has only happened once. Only Brewster ever came Home and stayed. The other friends eventually all had to go away.

Probably that is because all dogs are more wonderful than all other animals.

Except maybe Jax.

When I bent my head down, Nala rubbed the top of her head against my cheek. Jax opened one sleepy eye and his tail twitched, but that was his only reaction.

I realized in that moment just how much I loved this large kitten. She had come into the world afraid, but she had trusted me enough to play and tumble with me like any other cat, and now she was no longer timid and scared. I felt a little like I was the mother that Nala never had.

And now we were leaving each other. Nala and I stared at each other for a long, long moment, and then I returned to my girl.

Maggie Rose and Mom and I left the building and walked on the winding paths. Usually I was on my leash for this part, but this time Maggie Rose carried me and kept holding and hugging me. I didn't mind too much, even when we walked past a bit of pizza on the ground under a bush and I didn't get to go and eat it. It was so nice to have my girl be happy.

"I didn't want to tell you until I had permission from the zoo to try it out," Mom explained. "I didn't want to get your hopes up, Maggie Rose, in case they didn't want to try another dog instead of Lily. And then there was the question of whether Nala would accept a Rottweiler puppy. But they act like they've been friends their whole lives. It went even better than I was hoping."

"So Lily can really stay at home with us?" Maggie Rose asked, squeezing me a little tighter.

Mom put her arm around Maggie Rose's shoulders so we were all in the hug together. "Oh, yes, of course. Lily can stay."

We slipped into the car, and I curled up on Maggie Rose's lap in the back seat. I was tired from all my playing and a little sad, too, even though I was with my girl. I felt that something had gone away.

But my girl had not gone away, and that was what was most important.

"I bet Lily will miss Nala, though," Maggie

Rose said, stroking my back. "It's like she's lost her baby, kind of."

"We will all miss Nala," Mom said from the front of the car, which began moving.

"Lily is my baby," my girl proclaimed. "Are you my baby, Lily?"

Maggie Rose reached into an open bag that lay beside her on the seat. She pulled something out. It was a bottle, and it was full of milk! Maggie Rose flipped me onto my back, Brewster-style, and pulled me into her lap. I went willingly, my nose twitching.

She put the bottle near my face and I grabbed hold of the tip with my teeth quickly, before she could change her mind.

The milk that squirted into my mouth was rich and delicious and marvelous, just as I had always known it would be.

Sometimes it takes people a while to figure out what to do, but they usually get there in the end. Finally, Maggie Rose understood that bottles were not just for large cats—they were for good dogs, too.

And I was a very, very good dog.

MORE ABOUT AMUR LEOPARDS

All leopards have spots. They are called rosettes.

Leopards look a lot like jaguars, but you can tell the difference by looking at their spots. Jaguars have a spot in the center of each rosette. Leopards do not.

Leopards are nocturnal. They hunt at night and sleep or rest during the day, often up in trees.

Leopards are the smallest of the big cats. (The other big cats are lions, tigers, and jaguars.)

A leopard mother usually has two to three cubs at a time. They weigh a little more than one pound when they are born. The cubs stay with the mother for about two years, until they are old enough to hunt for themselves.

Wild leopards are found in Africa and Eurasia. Amur leopards, like Nala, live in eastern Russia and northern China. They are named after the Amur River, which runs along the border between the two countries.

Amur leopards usually live between ten to fifteen years in the wild. In a zoo, like Nala, one might live to be twenty.

Leopards are amazing jumpers. Amur leopards have been known to leap up to nineteen feet in one bound—that's like jumping over three adults lying head-to-toe on the ground.

All leopards are carnivores and eat meat.

Amur leopards hunt deer, wild pigs, mice, and rabbits.

Amur leopards are very endangered. There are fewer than a hundred left in the wild.

READ ON FOR A SNEAK PEEK AT
LILY TO THE RESCUE:
THE MISFIT DONKEY,
COMING SOON FROM STARSCAPE

"Oh, look, here comes Ringo! Doesn't he look handsome!"

The new arrival was a little like a horse, but he had a much longer neck and a smaller head. His fur was fuzzy and looked soft. His head was up so high, it was taller than even the taller of the two boys.

We get a lot of animals coming and going at Work, but this one was one of the strangest-looking. I was about to trot over to greet it and the new boys, but Maggie Rose called me and I went to her side, since that's what good dogs do.

"Is that a llama?" Bryan asked.

"Yep. Name's Ringo. Would you like to pet him? He was over at the neighbor's place, getting his coat groomed," Kelly replied.

"I saw him when I was here before. He didn't want to play with Lily," Maggie Rose added.

Kelly waved her hand. "Let Ringo loose, boys! And come on over."

The taller boy unclipped the horse-thing's leash and it immediately trotted over to where Scamper, Dash, and the donkey were still wrestling in the grass. All three stopped playing to see what this new animal would do.

The horse-thing ignored the pigs. It came right toward the little donkey, stamping with its hard hooves.

"Oh no!" Maggie Rose cried.

ABOUT THE AUTHOR

W. BRUCE CAMERON is the #1 *New York Times* bestselling author of *A Dog's Purpose, A Dog's Journey, A Dog's Way Home, A Dog's Promise;* the young-reader novels *Bailey's Story, Bella's Story, Ellie's Story, Lily's Story, Max's Story, Molly's Story, Shelby's Story, Toby's Story;* and the chapter-book series Lily to the Rescue. He lives in California.